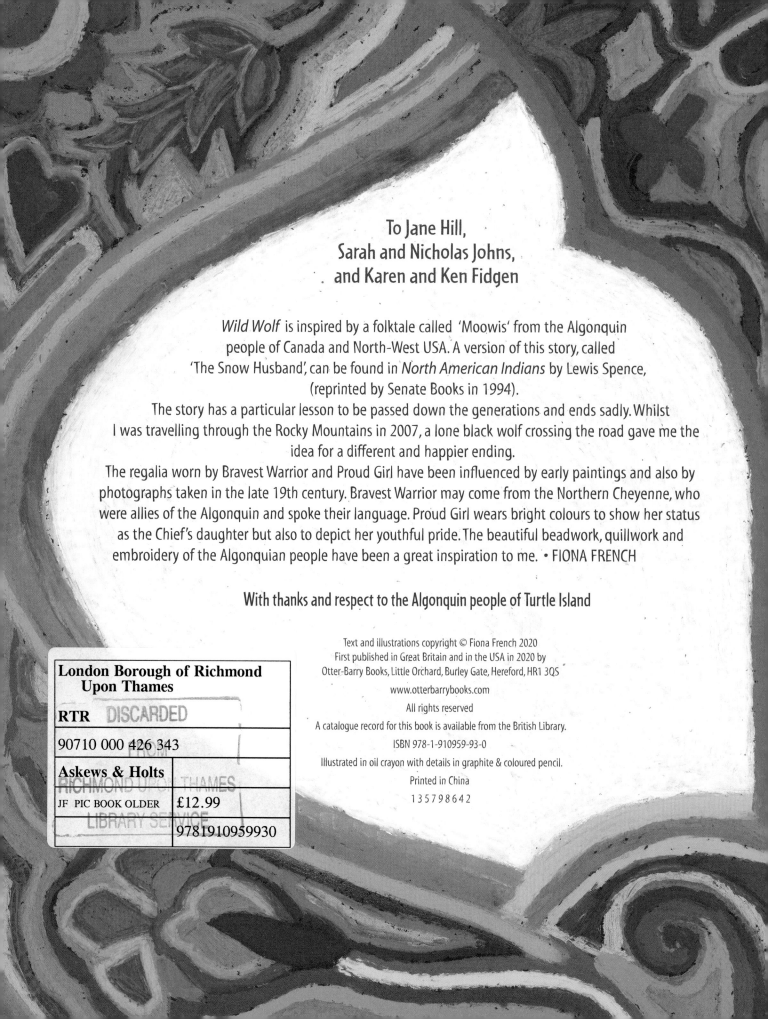

To Jane Hill,
Sarah and Nicholas Johns,
and Karen and Ken Fidgen

Wild Wolf is inspired by a folktale called 'Moowis' from the Algonquin
people of Canada and North-West USA. A version of this story, called
'The Snow Husband', can be found in *North American Indians* by Lewis Spence,
(reprinted by Senate Books in 1994).
The story has a particular lesson to be passed down the generations and ends sadly. Whilst
I was travelling through the Rocky Mountains in 2007, a lone black wolf crossing the road gave me the
idea for a different and happier ending.
The regalia worn by Bravest Warrior and Proud Girl have been influenced by early paintings and also by
photographs taken in the late 19th century. Bravest Warrior may come from the Northern Cheyenne, who
were allies of the Algonquin and spoke their language. Proud Girl wears bright colours to show her status
as the Chief's daughter but also to depict her youthful pride. The beautiful beadwork, quillwork and
embroidery of the Algonquian people have been a great inspiration to me. • FIONA FRENCH

With thanks and respect to the Algonquin people of Turtle Island

Text and illustrations copyright © Fiona French 2020
First published in Great Britain and in the USA in 2020 by
Otter-Barry Books, Little Orchard, Burley Gate, Hereford, HR1 3QS

www.otterbarrybooks.com

All rights reserved

A catalogue record for this book is available from the British Library.

ISBN 978-1-910959-93-0

Illustrated in oil crayon with details in graphite & coloured pencil.

Printed in China

1 3 5 7 9 8 6 4 2

WILD WOLF

INSPIRED BY AN ALGONQUIN FOLKTALE

Fiona French

Otter-Barry BOOKS

I am Wild Wolf,
   guardian spirit to the people who live in
   the high mountains.
      Many times, I have seen that danger is
      not outside in the forest,
         but inside humans ....

Long ago, a tribal chief
had a beautiful daughter.
She was very proud.
Brave warriors came from far and wide
to ask for her hand in marriage.
She refused them all.

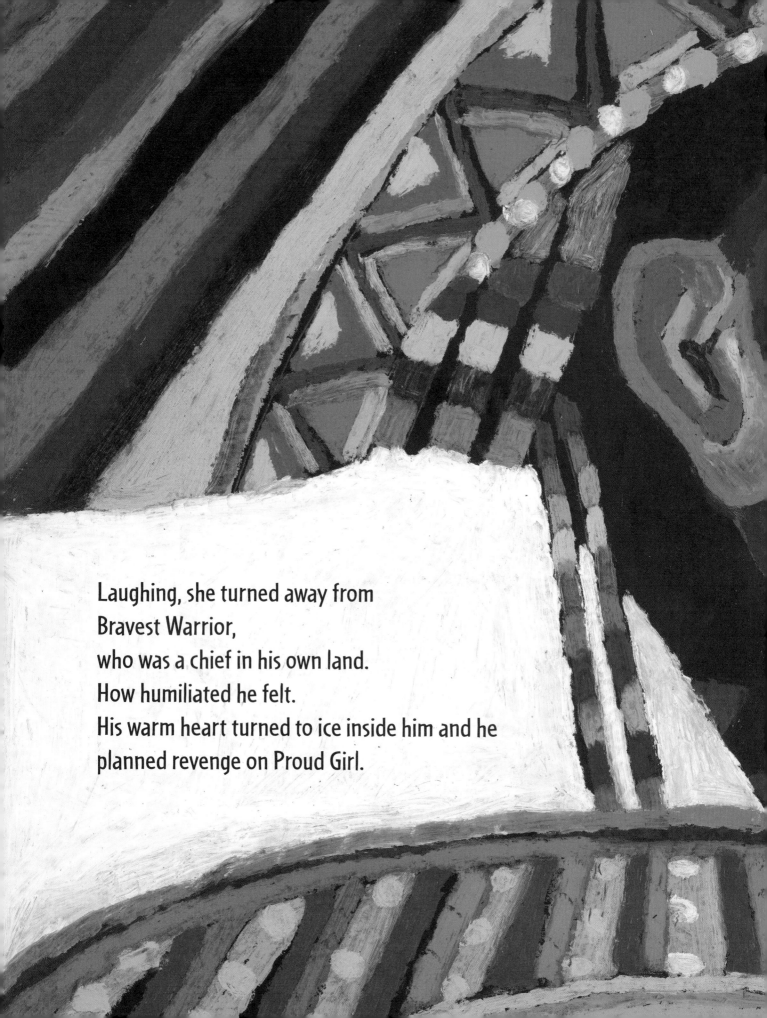

Laughing, she turned away from
Bravest Warrior,
who was a chief in his own land.
How humiliated he felt.
His warm heart turned to ice inside him and he
planned revenge on Proud Girl.

Bravest Warrior gathered up all the old rags and animal bones
that the tribe had thrown away.
With ice and snow he formed them into a shape of a man.
He covered it in his finest clothes
and Ice Man came alive.

Proud Girl saw Ice Man in the shadows,
far from the flames and the fire.
She loved him instantly, more
than anyone in the world.
The revenge of Bravest Warrior
closed in around her.

She married Ice Man
and followed him back to his tribal lands.
It was difficult keeping up with
her strange new husband.
He kept to the cold shadows.

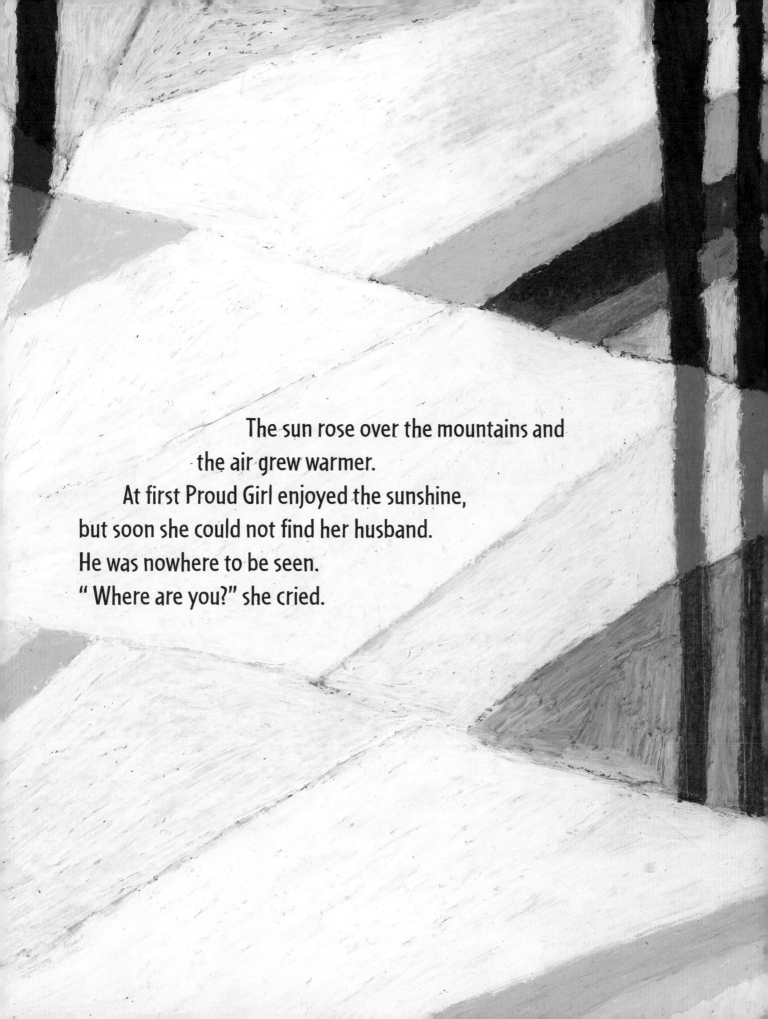

The sun rose over the mountains and
the air grew warmer.
At first Proud Girl enjoyed the sunshine,
but soon she could not find her husband.
He was nowhere to be seen.
" Where are you?" she cried.

She searched the forest for a long time and found him
melted away into the ground.
Nothing was left of handsome Ice Man but old bones and
the empty clothes of Bravest Warrior.

As night fell, Proud Girl sank
into a deep, cold sleep.
She would have died there
but I, Wild Wolf, could not let that happen.
With my strong jaws, I dragged
Ice Man's blanket over her
to keep her warm.

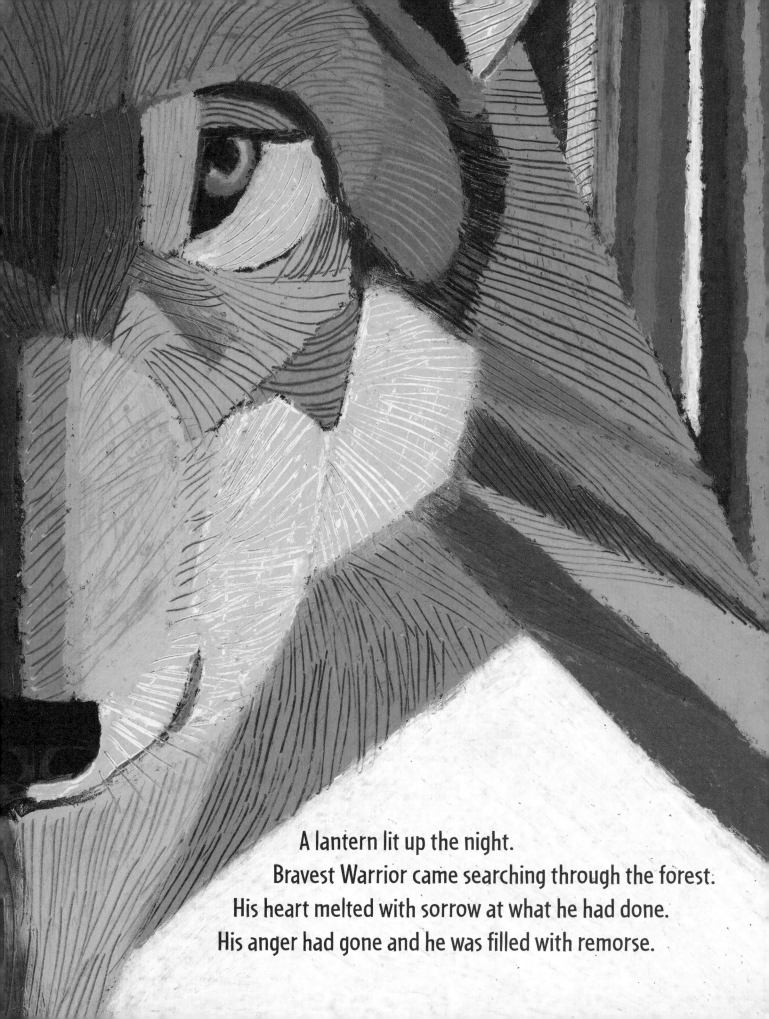

A lantern lit up the night.
Bravest Warrior came searching through the forest.
His heart melted with sorrow at what he had done.
His anger had gone and he was filled with remorse.

He built a fire and stayed with Proud Girl until morning.
She too had changed and was proud no more.
She went with Bravest Warrior to his homeland
by the Great Lake.

Watching over them,
I sometimes howl in the evening light,
rejoicing that humans can be kind and loving too.